The Arrest

A Swedish Crime Story

Stockholm Sleuth Series
(Prequel)

CHRISTER THOLIN

Content

THE ARREST

ars struggled to balance the tray of food from McDonalds as he got back into the police car. As he was doing so, his partner, Kalle, started the car.

"A radio message just came through for us. We have to head on over to Spånga. Damn, and this has to happen just when I'm starving."

Lars put on his seatbelt as the car took off, which made it difficult to keep the cups on the tray. He wanted to avoid getting any coffee stains on his clothes, even though they wouldn't have been very visible on the dark blue police uniform.

"You can still chow down your burger while driving. That is, if you would drive a little slower. So, what's the problem?"

"A code seven, suspected twenty-two. It's urgent."

Seven was the police code for a domestic incident, twenty-two for violence. Presumably it was a domestic quarrel that escalated, the type of incident where women were usually the victim.

"Familiar address?" Frequently, these were recurring cases where the man had already been repeatedly warned.

"No, a new one." Kalle switched on the blue light and activated the siren. He quickly drove past the other cars on the road before turning onto 275. They would need just a little more than five minutes to reach the address.

Lars was just as hungry as Kalle. They had been out since 7 that morning, but since he didn't have to do the driving, his hands were free, and he unwrapped his hamburger.

"Oh shit, that smell is driving me crazy. Open the window!"

"I can hand-feed you." Lars grinned.

"It'll happen one day. I may be a few years older than you, but I haven't reached that point yet by any means."

Lars cranked open the window with the handle and the squad car filled with fresh air. He bit into his hamburger. He would have to hurry if he wanted to finish eating it before they reached their destination. Once they took care of the problem, it would most certainly be cold.

Kalle activated the siren once again as he turned from the 275 onto Sörgårdsvägen. Other drivers stopped, pulled over and let them pass.

"That's right, everyone get out of the way," Kalle crooned contentedly.

The pace slowed down a bit on Sörgårdsvägen, because they had to go through several red traffic lights. Despite the blue light and siren being on, it's still necessary to be careful when going through a light when it's red. At one point they even had to wait a full minute for the stopped cars to pull to the side and form a tunnel wide enough for them to pass through. They then made a right turn into the residential area where their target destination was located. Beautiful Swedish mansions lined the streets, many in classic red, but also some in white, yellow and blue. The houses were on large lots, so there were also many trees and other types of foliage in between the homes. Many of the properties had flagpoles with the Swedish flag and these could be seen blowing in the wind. After making two more turns, Kalle stopped in front of a red house with the number 54 on it and turned the car off. The street was narrow and there was only enough room for two cars to pass each other. They both got out of the car. Kalle sent a radio message to dispatch letting them know that they had reached their destination and were now going to the house.

Lars had a look around. The house really stood out from the others in the neighborhood, because it looked run-down in comparison: the paint was peeling off, the windows looked old and the roof had definitely seen better times, a fact that was mercilessly exposed in the bright sunshine. On the grassy area in front of the house was a swing and a small soccer goal. The property was surrounded by a short fence that was painted red, with an opening between two brick pillars from which a metal gate was hanging. The gate was open, which allowed them access to the property. They walked along the narrow sandy path, passing by two children's bicycles. The path led directly to the main entrance of the house. The front door was located on the side of a porch. They quickly climbed the six concrete steps. Lars listened but could not hear any noises coming from inside the house. In these kinds of cases, often loud screaming could be heard. However, all that could be heard here was silence. Kalle rang the doorbell. An unpleasant buzzing could be heard coming from inside the house. How could anyone possibly tolerate listening to a doorbell ring that sounded like this all the time? Judging by how the rest of the house looked, though, the doorbell was probably the smallest of the problems the owners had. Kalle rang the doorbell again, but there was no reaction.

Lars pushed down on the handle and pulled the door. To his surprise, it wasn't locked and swung open, outwards as is customary in Sweden. He looked at Kalle, who nodded. Carefully they entered the house, which was dark inside.

"Hello. Is anyone home? This is the police," Kalle shouted into the house.

Now suddenly sounds could be heard. Further towards the back of the house, someone was moving and then something seemed to fall over. Then someone screamed. Lars drew his pistol. He saw Kalle had his hand on the grip, but his Sig Sauer was still in the holster. They swiftly moved down the hallway. A quick peek into the kitchen on the left, nobody was in there. In front of them was the living room. They heard a door open. The room was full – there was furniture and boxes everywhere, just a chaotic mess. The two policemen positioned themselves next to each other. By now, Kalle was also holding his gun in his hand. They secured both sides, but there was nobody to be seen.

"Hello? Is anyone here?" Kalle shouted once again. A moan was the answer. It came from the right back corner, where there was a big table. They made their way through all the items in the room; there were lots of utensils scattered around on the floor and

Lars stepped on a toy train, which rolled out from under him almost causing him to fall down. Once they reached the table, Lars saw to bare feet. Someone was lying on the floor.

"Lars, cover!" Kalle put his pistol back in the holster and knelt down next to the woman who was lying half under the table. Next to her was a large pool of blood.

Lars raised his service weapon and checked the living room again, but there was no one else in the room. He heard the woman moaning. Kalle had taken her hand and spoke to her. "Where are you hurt? Can you stand up?"

The woman just groaned, it didn't sound like the answer was "yes". Kalle turned on his radio and requested an ambulance be sent. Lars studied the woman. She was dressed only in a robe, which was not closed, and underneath it she only had on white briefs. Her skin showed numerous bruises, as well as some smaller bleeding wounds. Kalle was trying to cover her with the robe without moving her. Her face was severely battered, her eyes blue-red and swollen, her nose bleeding, her lips split open and her neck showing red strangulation marks. This was really one of the worst abuse cases he had ever encountered. However, Lars wondered where all the blood on the floor came from, because he couldn't see any injury that could account for it. Did she have a wound on her back or on the back of her head?

Then, right at that moment, the patio door behind him suddenly swung open and Lars immediately turned around. The door apparently had been left slightly ajar and a gust of wind, most likely blowing in from the front door, had caused it to open a crack.

Kalle noticed it as well. "The guy fled out the back door. Lars, will you pursue him? I'm calling for backup."

"Okay." Lars pushed the door open and stepped outside. On the other side of the back door was a stone terrace that had garden furniture strewn around. Beyond the terrace was a lawn that hadn't been mowed for some time and a few trees. Lars looked around, but he couldn't see anyone. The guy must have already run a bit further. He had either jumped the fence and fled to the neighboring property, or he had gone back around to the front of the house towards the street. Lars opted for the street. He ran around the left side of the house, but there was nobody to be seen out front, neither on the property or the street. He walked slowly to the police car, but continued to constantly look around, still holding his gun in firing position. Just as he reached the garden gate, he heard a car start a little further to the left behind the police car. He sprinted forward and was just in time to see a dark blue Mazda drive off in the direction they had just come from. He managed to make out just two letters on the license plate before the car had put too much distance between them to see it anymore.

"Shit," cursed Lars. He ran to the police car and yanked open the door on the driver's side. Typically, when they were called out on assignments like these, Kalle would leave the key in the ignition. Yes, he did today as well. Lars hastily got into the car and started it. He had his doubts as to whether he would be able to catch up with the Mazda, because he still had to turn around on the narrow road, but in any case, he would at least try. Two houses down there was a driveway. He pulled into it and was able to turn the car around in just a single maneuver. He then stepped on the gas and drove down the narrow road with the siren on, which he had set to sound continuously. Under no circumstances did he want to endanger a child playing on the street or an old woman. He contacted the central office to inform them that the suspect was on the run in a car and gave a description of that car's distinguishing features. Perhaps some fellow officers were nearby who could help him chase down the suspect.

He reached the first intersection, but the Mazda was nowhere to be seen. The driver must have made a turn. The only thing Lars could do was to guess which direction. He surmised that the suspect had most likely driven towards Sörgårdsvägen, because from there he could quickly reach 275 or even the highway E18. At least, that's what Lars would have done if he had been in the suspect's shoes. So, following that line of thought, he turned left and then made another left at the next intersection. Once he reached the Sörgårdsvägen traffic light, he stopped and got out of the car. He looked around, but the Mazda was nowhere to be seen. He had either not been fast enough to catch up or the Mazda's driver had chosen to drive through the small streets of the residential area and had come out somewhere else, for instance in Vällingby or Sundbyberg. In any case, there was no point searching for the suspect any further. He had lost him.

Lars got back into the car and turned off the siren, then drove back to the house. An ambulance was already parked in front of the house and Lars saw the woman being carried out on a gurney. They had arrived quickly. Kalle came out after the ambulance crew and sat down with Lars in the car.

"What happened? Did the guy get away?"

"Yeah. He took off in a car, but unfortunately in a different direction. By the time I turned the car around, he was already long gone. Did the woman say anything else?"

Kalle shook his head. "Nope, she was pretty out of it. They had to treat her right where she was, because she had a laceration on the back of her head that bled like crazy. She certainly has a concussion, if not worse. As far as I could determine, he hit her with the poker for the fireplace, which I secured. It's up to the forensics team to do the rest. Right now, I'm going to finally eat my hamburger before I keel over too."

Lars just grinned, because he could completely understand that. He watched Kalle bite into the burger, which at this point was certainly only lukewarm at best. However, that didn't stop Kalle from eating it in no time at all.

"So, what do we do now?" The ambulance had already left, and a second police car just arrived, which was surely the backup they had requested.

Kalle wiped his mouth with the back of his hand. "You can send them away. We're waiting for forensics. Apart from that, we should have a chat with headquarters. They need to take a look at the personal register data."

Lars exited the car and greeted the two officers that just arrived. He gave them a brief update on the situation, after which they drove off. At that point, the van with the people from the forensics squad pulled up. Lars briefed them on the situation as well and they consequently entered the house with their equipment. When Lars arrived back at the car, Kalle had already taken his place at the steering wheel again. He had just ended a call to headquarters.

"What did they say?"

"Well, Evelina Appell and Ulf Wallin live here. They're not married but are living together and have three children. She's 34, he's 38. He was once arrested for fighting, but he wasn't convicted for it. It is safe to assume that it was the two of them who had an argument here. Your description of the car that you were pursuing matches up with the car that belongs to Ulf Wallin, including the two letters you were able to catch from the license plate. Our orders are to first question the neighbors and then drive to the hospital to try and question our victim."

"Yeah, well, I guess we'll have to wait there for a while. Karolinska? Or where did they take her?"

"You got it. Yeah, I'm afraid so. There's nothing we can do about it." Kalle drank the last sip from his McDonalds cup, then they both got out of the car and split up.

***

Lars ran as fast as he could up the last steps leading to the third floor where their apartment was located. It was almost seven o'clock, once again time had flown by and it was getting late.

He unlocked the door and shouted, "Hello, anyone home?"

The bathroom door opened and his wife, Lisa, came out to happily greet him. "You're finally here, honey."

Lisa put her arms around him and give him a long, deep kiss on the mouth. Her large belly pressed against his groin. He could feel how it was arousing him and he tried to take his mind off of that by thinking of something else. Lately, Lisa had felt like cuddling a lot, but she didn't feel like having sex. That wasn't surprising considering her stomach – she was in the ninth month of her pregnancy.

"Sorry, took a little longer today. We had a serious case."

"You say that almost every day, honey."

Lars shrugged his shoulders. "What should I do? I'd also prefer to be home earlier."

Lisa smiled. "I know. Go change and come to the table. Dinner is already waiting."

"Great. I'm so hungry, I could eat a horse."

Ten minutes later, they were sitting at the table. Lisa had prepared the typical Thursday dinner consisting of pea soup with pieces of bacon and pancakes topped with jam and cream for dessert. The pea soup was quite hearty, and Lars had already eaten a large bowl of it.

"How are you doing today? You look really good." Lars looked at Lisa adoringly. She had been on sick leave for two weeks because of her pregnancy, but today she really looked radiant.

"Yeah, today was a good day. I went to the indoor swimming pool today and it really felt good. I didn't feel the extra weight in the water and I stayed in it for over half an hour." The gynecologist had given her this tip, but it was the first time that she had actually tried it out, even though Lars had urged her several times to go.

"Did you go alone?"

"No, I went together with Sanna, you know, the tall blonde from the pregnancy exercise group."

Lars nodded that he remembered. He had a guilty conscience because he had only managed to go to the exercise class with her twice, but it started at six in the evening and most of the time, work kept him from going.

"That's good. How's she doing?"

"Good. She's got a month more to go. She's still working and goes regularly to the exercise sessions."

Lars scraped every bit of soup out of the bowl.

"Do you want some more?"

"*Nej*, now it's time for the pancakes." Lars grinned.

Lisa handed him a new plate and put a pancake on it. Lars put two spoonfuls of jam and a heaping spoonful of whipped cream on top of it. He then spread it all over the pancake so that it was covered in a red and white spread.

"So, tell me. What was the case today?"

"Oh, we were called out to a single-family home in Spånga for a reported domestic dispute. The woman was violently assaulted, taken to Karolinska Hospital where she is now and she's still not in any condition to be questioned." The doctor had not allowed Lars and his colleagues to see the woman that day, because she still hadn't regained consciousness. They would have to try again tomorrow.

"What did her boyfriend do to her?" Lisa looked at him with her eyes wide open. Lars was uncertain about how many details he should share with her. He was always thrilled that she showed an interest in his cases, but he also noticed many times that she couldn't deal very well with the brutality and dangers that came along with his job. That hadn't exactly improved with the pregnancy.

He looked at her with a solemn expression on his face. "He beat her up big time. She had bruises all over her body and a severe concussion." He chose to omit the fact that a fireplace poker had been used.

"Oh my God, how awful. How can a man do that to his own wife? What was the fight about?"

"We don't know that yet, but we hope the woman can tell us something tomorrow."

"And her boyfriend isn't saying anything either?"

"Him? We haven't caught him yet. He took off when we showed up."

"I see. Well, at least he didn't attack you. Otherwise it might have turned into a dangerous situation for you too."

"Lisa, there's two of us and we both go in with our guns drawn and ready to use. He wouldn't have stood a chance."

Lars ate another piece of his pancake, which was really delicious. He loved Thursdays.

"And the boyfriend didn't come back? Does he even live in the house?"

"He does. He lives there with her. In front of the house we have officers keeping guard, but he'll probably go somewhere else to hide out."

"Has he beaten his wife many times before this?"

"Not that we know of. The neighbors couldn't tell us anything such either."

Lisa just shook her head, not able to comprehend how something like that could happen. "How can an argument spiral out of control like that? Do the two have any children?"

"Yes, three kids. One goes to kindergarten, the other two were in school."

"What happens to them now? When both of their parents aren't there."

"We called social services and they take care of it. If there are no relatives who can take care of the children, they'll be placed in foster care."

"How horrible for the children. They leave for school and kindergarten in the morning and then when evening rolls around, they can't go home and see their parents."

Lars nodded. Fortunately, as police officers they didn't have to take care of the children. He was also happy, though, that the kids had not witnessed the fight, because that would have probably made things even worse.

Lisa motioned with the pancake plate and Lars took a second one. Today, he had certainly earned it. What's the old saying? Sugar soothes nerves.

"So, what happens now?"

"Tomorrow we'll search for the guy, in case he doesn't show up again or maybe even turn himself in."

"Just be careful. Soon, we'll be a complete family. We need you." Lisa stroked her belly in a demonstrative manner.

"I know, honey. I promise." Lars knew that Lisa worried every day, especially now that she wasn't working and spent most of the day alone at home. He decided to change the subject. "So, how's the house hunting going?"

Their apartment was small. There was only a tiny bedroom and a living room with a kitchenette. As long as the baby was small, it would work out. However, eventually they would need a room for their child. That's why they had already started looking for a house. Almost every weekend they were out to take a look at some properties, but so far, they've had no luck. The housing market in Stockholm was definitely a seller's market. The supply was low, but the prices high. You had to bid on a home and whenever they had placed a bid, the selling price always went up too high.

"There are a few new properties up for sale in the northwest, two in Vällingby and three in Hässelby. We should go take a look at some of them, but we'll have to wait two weeks before we can go tour them in person."

Lisa had grown up in Hässelby and wanted to live in that area. That wasn't ideal for Lars, because he always had to commute to Kungsholmen in the city for work. However, he also realized that they couldn't afford the centrally located homes.

"Great. I'll drink a cup of coffee now and then you can show me what's for sale."

Lisa stood up and was happy. "Yes, I would love that. The coffee is already brewed. Afterwards we'll settle down and get comfortable!"

***

he rain was pouring down. Obviously, the nice summer weather had come to an end. The next few days were going to be rainy as well, and on the cool side. Typical Swedish June weather.

Lars and Kalle hurried from the parking lot to the entrance of the Karolinska Hospital. After going through the big glass door, they headed straight to reception and asked to see Evelina Appell. Once they knew the station and room number where she was staying, they made their way to the elevator. The doctor had called that morning and informed them that Evelina was now fit to be questioned. That's why they went directly to her room. Kalle opened the door and inside the room they saw three beds. One bed was empty, the second was occupied by an old woman who was sleeping at the moment and in the third bed, which was in the back by the window, was Evelina. They each grabbed a chair and sat down beside the bed.

Evelina did not look much better than she did yesterday. Her face was still swollen with black and blues, small band-aids were covering wounds in several places and she had a bandage wrapped around her head, which presumably was covering the laceration on the back of her head. She wore a nightgown from the hospital, which was surely covering even more bandages. She sat up as they entered the room.

"*Hej*, Evelina," Kalle began. "We found you in your home yesterday after one of your neighbors called us. How are you doing?"

Evelina nodded her head to greet them. "I'm doing okay."

"Has social services come yet about your children?"

"Yes, tomorrow they're going to my sister's."

"Well, that's a good solution." Kalle quickly glanced at Lars and gave him a nod. This was important information, because now they knew there was a sister nearby.

"Obviously, we would like to know what happened yesterday. Can you tell us what was going on?"

She just stared at him with a blank look on her face, then shook her head. "I can't remember. I must have fallen."

Kalle leaned back. "I don't believe that. Your injuries indicate that you were beaten, and your neighbor said that there was an argument going on in your house."

"I don't know." Evelina laid her head down on the pillow.

Lars was surprised that the woman obviously didn't want to incriminate her boyfriend. That often was the case with women who were beaten regularly, but in this case, it seemed more like a first-time occurrence. Also, the suspect had severely battered her, and Lars had anticipated that she therefore would press charges against him.

He made another attempt. "Your boyfriend was there and fled. I tried to stop him, but he drove away in his car. Why did he leave you there seriously injured? Can you explain that?"

"I have no idea." She closed her eyes. "I'm tired and have a headache. I want to sleep now." She turned away from them.

Lars looked at Kalle, who just shrugged his shoulders.

Lars asked her one final question. "Has your boyfriend contacted you?"

Evelina mumbled something that sounded like a "no". Lars gave up. They probably weren't going to get anything more out of her. Kalle wished her a speedy recovery and announced that they would be coming back again tomorrow. They said goodbye and left the room.

"Great", Lars said. "Should we admire or condemn her? Is it mistaken loyalty or fear?"

Kalle shook his head. "Probably a combination of all the above. It's not the first time something like this has happened and yet I still just don't understand it."

"Do you think she's been hit before?"

"It's hard to say. There's no evidence of something like this happening before. No information about similar injuries and the neighbors weren't aware of anything either."

They stepped into the elevator. "So, what do we do now?" asked Lars.

Kalle scratched the back of his head. "I need a cup of coffee. I'm going to the cafeteria. In the meantime, you can call the social worker and find out who the sister is. We should definitely go see her. Should I get you a coffee too?"

"*Nej*, thanks. Not right now. I'll go call social services."

"Good. Also, ask where the sister works. She probably won't be at home during our work hours."

Lars sought out a quiet corner in the hospital's reception area and called the number provided by headquarters this morning - cooperation between the agencies was considered paramount. The lady answered right away. She was very helpful and gave him the information he needed. He then joined Kalle in the cafeteria. Maybe he should have a cup of coffee after all.

***

t was still raining. They were driving south on the highway. Before that, they had eaten lunch at a rest stop. Kalle had apparently eaten enough, because he was humming contentedly.

They had met the sister where she was working. Her name was Margit and she worked as a saleswoman in the women's fashion department at the NK department store downtown. She had been much more talkative than Evelina and had told them immediately that there had already been several incidents in which Ulf had become physical with Evelina, but until now it had always been slaps and some lighter blows. It had never been as bad as was this time. Apparently, every time it was about money problems; when Ulf was unemployed, he would be in a bad mood and extremely irritable. A week ago, he had lost his job once again and must have just snapped yesterday.

Margit also had an idea of where Ulf might be hiding out. Her parents had a vacation home near Nyköping, which was used by both Margit and Evelina's family every summer and for which both sisters had the key.

At the same time, the colleagues working in the headquarters in Kungsholmen were able to locate Ulf's mobile phone. The location of the ping was a perfect match for the address of the vacation cottage. Although Ulf didn't answer when he was called, he had apparently failed to shut the phone off completely which made it possible for them to locate him. Now Kalle and Lars were on their way to the summer house, about a two-hour drive from Stockholm.

A little past Nyköping they turned onto the state road 53, which they followed for a while until they had to continue on a smaller road. Lars had entered the coordinates of the located mobile phone directly into the navigation system, so all they had to do now was follow the instructions, and that made it easier for them as the roads became narrower and narrower and they had to make more and more turns. Eventually, they arrived at the address. It was a large, hilly property with many trees and left mostly in its natural state. The house stood further back, only the red tiled roof shimmered between the trees. Kalle parked the police car in front of the entrance to the property and looked at Lars.

"I hope he hasn't parked his car somewhere else so he can get away from us again."

"There's no one parked here on the road, that's certain. He's got his car on the property, provided he's even here and not gone somewhere else already."

Kalle nodded. Lars looked down the driveway. The path leading to the house made a bend behind a big rock, perhaps Ulf's car was behind it.

"Well, let's go find out." Kalle opened his door.

Kalle and Lars walked slowly down the path towards the rock. Luckily, the rain had stopped. Kalle notified headquarters that they had now arrived at their destination and were preparing to make an arrest. They were both fully equipped, and further to the weapon on their belts hung an extra magazine of ammunition, a two-way radio, a mobile phone, a lockpick and handcuffs. Even though the man had fled after their last encounter, they were hoping that he had come to his senses in the meantime and would let himself be taken into custody without incident. Nonetheless, Lars was feeling uneasy. There was no way of knowing how an arrest would go down.

Cautiously they circled around the big rock. Lars had his hand on his service weapon, while Kalle seemed less worried. And indeed, there was the Mazda, parked right in front of the house. A single-story vacation home painted a dark color with white window frames. They walked past the Mazda towards the front door.

Lars was just contemplating whether they should separate and one of them should go around to the back of the house, when a loud bang pierced the silence. Kalle screamed and then collapsed. Lars threw himself down to the ground and pulled out his gun. He surveyed the house and saw a window to the left of the front door that was open, but he could not see anyone in it. Slowly he turned to Kalle. He was holding his side and his face was distorted with pain.

"Damn it, he got me," he moaned.

Lars turned to look at the house again, but there was no sign of movement. He crawled to Kalle and carefully pulled him behind the Mazda, so they were both out of the line of fire.

"How bad is it?" he asked Kalle.

Kalle lifted his hand up and blood poured out of the wound above the belt.

"Oh, shit," Lars cursed. It didn't look good.

Kalle pressed his hand back on the wound and gave Lars an intense look: "Go get the guy, Lars."

"Yeah, but what about you? You need a doctor."

"I'll call for one myself. I'll be fine." Lars looked at him uncertainly. Should he really leave him alone?

"Go now! Otherwise he'll get away again."

Lars stood up and looked over the car towards the house. There was still no one to be seen. The shooter had most likely retreated further back into the house, possibly already on the run. Lars ducked behind the Mazda and made his way to the front bumper. He heard Kalle talking to headquarters over the radio. They would certainly dispatch an ambulance and backup, probably from Nyköping, which would take a while. Oh well, in that case he would have to arrest the guy and then take care of Kalle. There were plenty of first-aid supplies in the police car.

Lars crawled out from behind the car and was about to sprint to the front door when all of a sudden there was movement in the open window. He still saw the muzzle flash before taking cover again. The shot then hit the ground next to him, causing the earth to spatter in all directions. The guy apparently had a rifle and must have remained at the window after all. All the better, because Lars could apprehend him there, assuming he managed to even get into the house.

"I'll cover you." Kalle was obviously was not going down easy.

Lars got back on his feet and readied himself. There were already shots fired. Kalle aimed at the open window, the bullets hit right and left of it. Lars ran off and reached the door unharmed. He pushed down the handle. Damn, it was locked. Maybe it was a better idea anyway if he went in through the back.

He turned to the right and ran around the house. The sidewall had two windows, at which he crouched down so as not to be seen in case the shooter had these windows in his sight. Once he had reached the rear corner of the house, he stopped to get his bearings and study his surroundings. There was a large wooden terrace with lots of garden furniture. The patio door was open – luckily. However, the wall from the corner to the door was completely made of glass, but he had no choice but to take this risk. At that moment, he heard more shots. They must have come from Kalle's pistol. Good ol' Ulf had probably reappeared at the window and was hopefully occupied. This was his chance. He rushed to the patio door and charged into the room where he threw himself behind a large sofa. Another shot – this time it sounded like it came from Ulf's rifle. At the side of the living room where Lars was now located, there was a hallway leading straight to the front door. There were two doors on the right and two on the left. Ulf had to be behind the last door on the right.

Lars decided to give the man one last chance.

"Ulf Wallin, surrender now! There is no way out for you. You can't escape and backup is already on the way. This is your last chance to get out of here safely. Put your rifle away and stand with your hands up, then nothing will happen to you."

Lars listened, hoping that Ulf would respond, because he wasn't particularly keen on shooting at the man, even if he had injured his partner. At first it was quiet, but then he suddenly heard quick movements. He saw the man running down the hallway and disappearing into one of the rooms on the other side. Although Lars still had his gun raised, the man had been too fast. Lars jumped up, assuming that Ulf was going to escape through one of the windows and then flee across the neighboring properties. He didn't want it to come to that. He sprinted to the far door where Ulf had bolted to. Pointing his pistol to the front, he made a rapid twisting motion through the door frame, ensuring that most of his body was covered.

He had expected to see the man at the window, but instead the room appeared empty. It was a children's room – a bunk bed on the right wall, a small table in front of the window, toys on the floor. Lars hesitated, baffled as there was no place for a grown man to hide. The window was locked, the latches were secured from the inside. Had he been wrong, had Ulf fled to the other room? At that moment he heard noises coming from his left. He turned around and saw a narrow door recessed into the wall right next to the corner of the room. It had to be a closet. Lars positioned himself next to the small door and yanked it open. To his amazement he looked through the closet past hanging clothes into the adjoining room. Then he heard Ulf running down the hallway towards the living room. Damn, what a dirty trick. The closet was accessible from both rooms and Ulf had used it as an escape route. Lars turned around and ran back through the door into the hallway. He was just in time to see Ulf leave the house through the patio door. He lifted his gun and fired. The shots didn't seem to have hit, because Ulf kept running from the terrace over the lawn. Lars followed him and when he arrived at the patio door, the fugitive was halfway across the lawn, on his way to a small shed. Lars stopped, stood up with his legs apart and aimed at the man's back, holding the pistol with both hands. The shot was fired, and Ulf collapsed on the lawn.

"Don't move," Lars shouted and approached cautiously, keeping his pistol in a firing position.

When he was within six feet of him, Ulf suddenly flipped over and fired the rifle at him. Lars also pressed the trigger and fired twice. At that moment, he felt a burning pain in his knee, his leg collapsed under him and he fell to his side. His pistol was still pointed at Ulf and when he hit the ground, another shot was fired. He watched as Ulf's body jerked.

They were both on their sides, facing each other. Ulf was bleeding from several gunshot wounds, he was either unconscious or dead, the rifle was in front of him on the grass. Lars looked at his leg, it was bleeding heavily and the pain was unbearable. Holy shit, he seemed to have hit him bad. He reached for his radio.

***

isa had just left the room again. He had already been in hospital for three days. They operated on him immediately after he was admitted into the hospital. Kalle was still in intensive care, the shot to his abdomen had led to an infection and his condition was still critical. However, it appeared he would make it.

The doctor had told Lars that the shot had gone straight through his knee, which unfortunately had caused serious damage. The doctors had patched everything up as well as they possibly could, and the operation had been successful. They were unable to fully rebuild his knee, though, and a certain amount of stiffness would probably persist indefinitely, even after six months of rehabilitation.

The chief had come to visit yesterday and had praised him for his work. It was very unusual for someone to attack two police officers with a rifle over an offense as minor as bodily injury and, in the opinion of his boss, it was really not to be expected. Otherwise, of course, he would have sent a larger team out. Ulf Wallin did not survive, Lars had hit him four times in the chest. There would be an internal investigation, but his boss was sure that this was just a formality, he was convinced that Lars had acted correctly, and the shooting was justified. Ultimately, the man had opened fire first, seriously injured one policeman and then also shot Lars. The chief had wished him all the best for his recovery and recommended that he take full advantage of the rehabilitation program. They would be happy to take him back into service afterwards.

That was the part that Lars didn't like at all. When he had talked about the stiffening of the knee, his boss had immediately become serious and had talked about starting to work behind the desk. He had also remained firm on Lars' insistence that he absolutely wanted to do field work again and had linked this to the complete rehabilitation of the knee. Desk work was out of the question for Lars. He loved driving in a patrol car, the action while on duty. All the paperwork stuff wasn't really his thing.

When he had complained about this to Lisa, she was nearly thrilled about it.

"Then you won't have to face these dangerous situations anymore, Lars," she had beamed. "And the hours of duty are certainly much more regular than in the field."

Of course, she was sorry about the knee and the resulting disability, but she liked the prospect of a transfer. Rehab was also good for them, she said – so Lars could experience the first weeks at home with the child instead of being on duty all the time.

Although Lars could understand where she was coming from and had to admit that it would certainly be nice to be with Lisa and the baby after the birth, she still couldn't get him to warm up to the idea of having desk duty. He would do everything in his power to restore full function to his leg in rehab, perhaps the reassignment could still be averted after all. Yes, that's what he had to do, that was the best option. First, he had to be discharged from the hospital, then he had to go through the rehabilitation process, spend time with the baby and finally return to patrol duty.

Lars leaned back, not all was lost yet.

THANKS TO THE READER

I am thrilled that you have read my book. I especially hope that you liked it.

You can let me know directly what you thought about the book! Your feedback is extremely important to me – this way I get the chance to consider the preferences of my readers.

contact@christertholin.one
www.christertholin.one

My heartfelt thanks
Christer Tholin

ABOUT THE AUTHOR

The author is originally from Schleswig-Holstein in Germany and has lived for many years with his family in Stockholm / Sweden, where he works as an independent management consultant.

He is a great fan of Swedish crime literature and had been planning for a long time to make his own contribution. That has already come to fruition with his first book, "VANISHED?" which is also the first book of the "Stockholm Sleuth Series" introducing Elin and Lars. "SECRETS?" is their second case.

www.christertholin.one

VANISHED?

Stockholm Sleuth Series, Book 1
By Christer Tholin
2016, Stockholm

She: a very hot 30 something Swedish woman. ***He:*** a native of Berlin, on vacation in rural Sweden, seeking solace for his broken heart. They meet. He finds her irresistible. But before their relationship can get off the ground, she vanishes mysteriously, having apparently been abducted. So Martin sets out to rescue Liv from her captors, with the aid of two Swedish detectives in a race against time – and across Sweden. In so doing, Martin and his intrepid detective duo put their very lives on the line.

https://www.amazon.com/gp/product/B071KYQ2XZ/

SECRETS?

Stockholm Sleuth Series, Book 2
By Christer Tholin
2017, Stockholm

In the crime novella SECRETS?, fledgling private investigator Elin Bohlander takes on what looks like an easy assignment — at first: to determine if her client's boyfriend is having an affair with another woman. To do this, Elin follows him to a secluded cabin in the woods, where she soon discovers that what's actually transpiring is stranger than anyone thought. Having ventured too far, she's stumbled upon a hornet's nest and put her life at risk. But it's too late. Can Elin win the unequal fight against a gang of brutal child molesters?

https://www.amazon.com/gp/product/B075VWXGHN/

MURDER?

Stockholm Sleuth Series, Book 3
By Christer Tholin
2019, Stockholm

Christina's idyllic existence with her husband Patrik comes to an abrupt end when Patrik suddenly vanishes from their suburban home in Stockholm.
At her wits end, she contacts local sleuths Lars and Elin, who ultimately trace Patrik's movements to the wooded wilds of northern Sweden, but too late – he's found dead. The police rule his death an accident, but Christina thinks otherwise – and so she asks Lars and Elin to do a thorough investigation of the circumstances surrounding Patrik's demise. Was his death really accidental, or was foul play involved? And was the mysterious Natalia somehow implicated?

https://www.amazon.com/dp/B07J9HZK23/